For Gemk,

Whose endless supply of ideas and honest critique made this possible.

感謝 Gemk

源源不絕的靈感及誠懇的建議讓這一切成真。

The Werewolf

我的朋友是狼人

Coleen Reddy　著

周　旭　繪

薛慧儀　譯

三民書局

Walter loved walking in the woods at night.
He always tried to spot owls that were nocturnal and could only be seen at night.
But he only walked in the woods when there was a full moon so that there was lots of light.

華特喜歡在晚上到森林去散步，試著尋找貓頭鷹的蹤影，
因為牠們是夜行性動物，只有在晚上才能見到。
但是他只在滿月的時候去森林，因為這樣才有充足的光線。

3

One night as he started walking home, he noticed something in his path.
It looked like a wolf, but it was standing on two legs like a person!
It howled loudly and started moving towards Walter.

有天晚上他正要從森林走回家時，發現路上有個奇怪的東西。
牠看起來像狼，卻像人一樣用兩隻腳站著！
牠大聲地長嘯，並往華特的方向移動。

5

Walter turned and ran, but when he looked up, the strange thing he had seen was standing in front of him again. "What are you? What do you want with me?" asked Walter. But Walter already knew what it was. The full moon and all the howling meant one thing. It was a **werewolf!**

華特轉身就跑，但他一抬頭，就看見那奇怪的傢伙又站在他面前。
「你到底是什麼東西？你想要做什麼？」華特問。
但華特已經知道那是什麼了。滿月和狼嚎，意味著⋯⋯狼人！

Walter started screaming for help.
Walter closed his eyes and he tried to
get free of the werewolf's grip.

華特開始大叫求救。

他閉上眼睛，試著想掙脫狼人的爪子。

9

Just as Walter thought he might faint with fear,
he felt the werewolf's grip loosen and the howling stopped.
Walter opened his eyes and instead of a werewolf,
he found himself facing a boy a little older than himself.

就在華特以為自己快要嚇暈時，
他發現狼人鬆開了爪子，也停止了嚎叫。
華特張開眼，發現站在眼前的不是狼人，
而是一個比自己稍微大一點的男孩。

11

The boy blinked a few times and then asked, "Where am I? Who are you?"
"You just tried to *kill* me," yelled Walter in an angry voice.
"You were a vicious werewolf a minute ago."

男孩眨眨眼，問道：「這是哪裡？你是誰？」
「你剛才想要殺我呢！」華特生氣地叫著。
「你剛剛還是一隻可惡的狼人呢！」

"Not again," cried the boy. "I can't live like this. My name is John. I used to be a regular kid, but then about a few months ago, strange things started happening whenever there was a full moon."

「怎麼又發生了！」男孩哭了起來。「我不能再這樣下去了。
我叫約翰，以前是個正常的小孩，可是大概從幾個月前開
始，只要一到滿月，就會發生奇怪的事。」

"I don't remember what happens when I turn into a werewolf. All I know is that I wake up to find myself about to hurt someone. I'm afraid that one day I might really hurt someone."

「我不記得變成狼人時所發生的事，只知道每次清醒時，
都發現我正好要去傷害別人！我好怕有天我真的會傷了人。」

"Isn't there something that you can do?" asked Walter.
"What can I do? The doctor won't believe me, and I'm afraid
my friends will think that I am a freak," John replied sadly.

「你一點辦法都沒有嗎?」華特問。
「我能怎麼辦呢?醫生不會相信我的,而且我怕
朋友們會認為我是個怪胎。」約翰難過地回答。

"I know someone who can help. There's a witch living in these woods. I could take you to her," offered Walter.
He felt sorry for John.

「我知道有人可以幫你。森林裡住了一個女巫，
我可以帶你去找她。」
華特提出這樣的建議，因為他很同情約翰的遭遇。

They found the witch's house and knocked on the door.
An old woman with white hair opened the door.
"What do you want?" asked the witch.

他們找到了女巫的家，然後敲了敲門。

一個白髮的老婆婆開了門。

「你們有什麼事嗎？」女巫問。

Walter told her all about John's being a werewolf.
"When the next full moon comes, you must go to the magic waterfall.
You must wash your face in the waterfall. When your body becomes two,
say this spell," said the witch, giving them a piece of paper.

華特把約翰變成狼人的事告訴了她。

「下次滿月的時候，你得去魔法瀑布洗臉。當你的身體變成
兩個後，就念這個咒語。」女巫說著，遞給他們一張紙。

25

During the next full moon, Walter and John met at the magic waterfall.
John stepped in and washed his face.

下一次滿月到來的時候，華特和約翰在魔法瀑布旁見面。
約翰踏進瀑布裡，開始洗臉。

Walter stared in disbelief as John's body divided into two separate things: the werewolf and John. The werewolf started fighting with John before he could say the spell.

The paper which the spell was written on fell into the water.

華特不敢相信地瞪大眼睛，看著約翰的身體真的變成了兩個：
一個是狼人，一個是約翰！
但在約翰還沒來得及念咒語前，狼人就和約翰打了起來。
結果寫著咒語的紙條掉進水裡了！

The werewolf was strangling John.

"*Help me,*" he screamed. Walter rushed into the water and found the piece of paper with the spell on it. He started to read:

"Wicked werewolf, let me be.
Leave my body. You can't live in me."

狼人緊緊地掐著約翰的脖子。

「救命呀！」他大叫著。華特趕忙跑進水裡，找到那張寫著咒語的紙條，念出咒語：「邪惡的狼人呀！還我本來面貌，快快離開我的身體！你不能住在我體內！」

Immediately, the werewolf disappeared.
John and Walter started walking home.
"I wasn't afraid of that stupid werewolf.
Did you see how I fought it?" John said.
"Yeah, I wasn't afraid of the werewolf either,"
replied Walter.

狼人馬上就消失了。約翰和華特於是開始走回家。
約翰說：「其實我一點也不怕那隻笨狼人，
你有看到我是多麼勇猛地和牠打鬥嗎？」
「嗯，我也不怕那隻狼人！」華特回答說。

Suddenly, they heard the howling of a wolf in the distance.
Without saying a word, they both started running home.

突然，他們聽到遠方傳來了狼嚎聲。
兩個人一句話也沒說，馬上就一溜煙地跑回家了！

35

狼人的家

1. 盒子（鞋盒或面紙盒）
2. 剪刀
3. 彩色筆
4. 膠水
5. 蒐集的小裝飾品或小東西
6. 線
7. 圖畫紙

＊在做勞作之前，要記得在桌上先鋪一張紙或墊板，
　才不會把桌面弄得髒兮兮喔！

步　驟

1. 將圖畫紙剪成與盒子內部三面一樣大。
2. 在圖畫紙上畫出森林的背景。
3. 將圖畫紙黏到盒子裡面。
4. 再用你所蒐集到的小東西裝飾在盒子裡。
5. 可以畫一些小裝飾品，再用線吊在盒子上端，狼人的
　 家就完成了。

　　　　另外，只要你有機會蒐集到像小貝殼、沙子、
　　　小花兒等東西，你也可以試著做沙灘、海底世
　　　界、花園等等的其他風景喔！

你可以將這裡附的狼人和其他人物剪下來，放在你做好的狼人的家裡呦！

生字表

39

國家圖書館出版品預行編目資料

The Werewolf:我的朋友是狼人 / Coleen Reddy著;
周旭繪; 薛慧儀譯.－－初版一刷.－－臺北市;
三民，2003
　　面; 公分－－(愛閱雙語叢書.二十六個妙朋
友系列) 中英對照
ISBN 957-14-3756-5 　(精裝)

1.英國語言－讀本

523.38　　　　　　　　　　　　92008819

© 　**The Werewolf**
──我的朋友是狼人

著作人　Coleen Reddy
繪　圖　周　旭
譯　者　薛慧儀
發行人　劉振強
著作財　三民書局股份有限公司
產權人　臺北市復興北路386號
發行所　三民書局股份有限公司
　　　　地址 / 臺北市復興北路386號
　　　　電話 / (02)25006600
　　　　郵撥 / 0009998-5
印刷所　三民書局股份有限公司
門市部　復北店 / 臺北市復興北路386號
　　　　重南店 / 臺北市重慶南路一段61號
初版一刷　2003年7月
編　號　S 85656-1
定　價　新臺幣壹佰捌拾元整
行政院新聞局登記證局版臺業字第○二○○號